Nora's Castle

Satomi Ichikawa

Philomel Books

NEW YORK

From Nora's house, in the village, you could easily see the castle. No one had lived in the old castle for a long time. "There may even be ghosts there," people told her. When it was stormy, or on gloomy winter days, you could really believe what they said. But when the weather was fine, how beautiful the castle looked! Was it really true that no one lived there? One day during summer vacation, Nora decided to find out for herself. With her constant companions, Maggie the doll, Teddy the stuffed bear, and Kiki the dog, she set out on her bicycle. The four explorers were in high spirits. What an adventure!

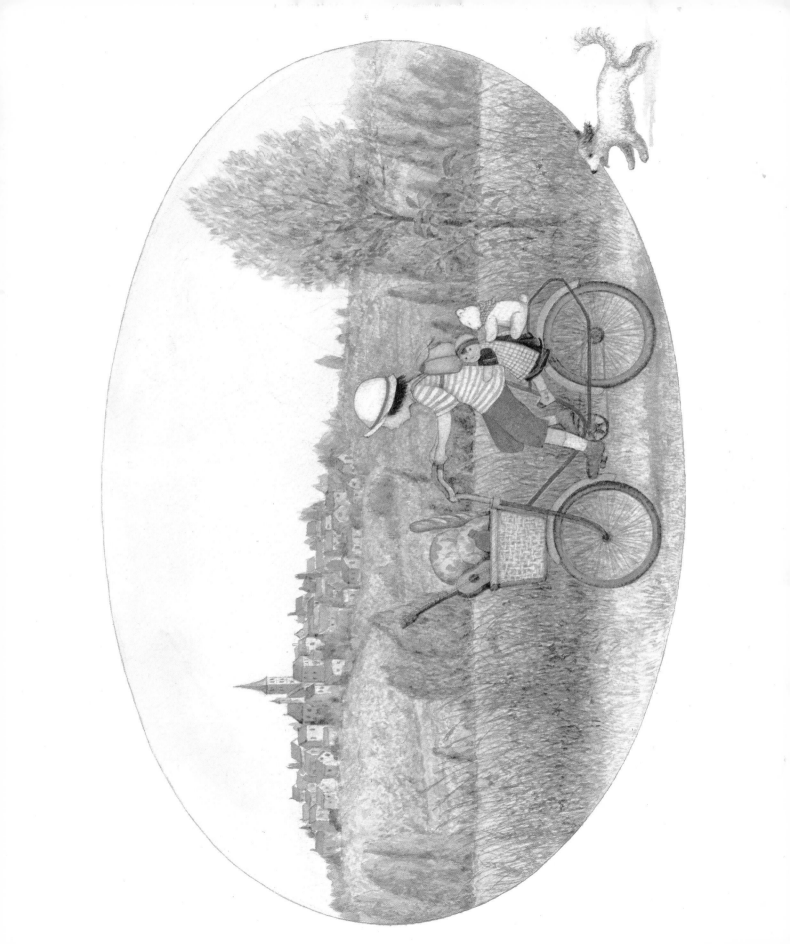

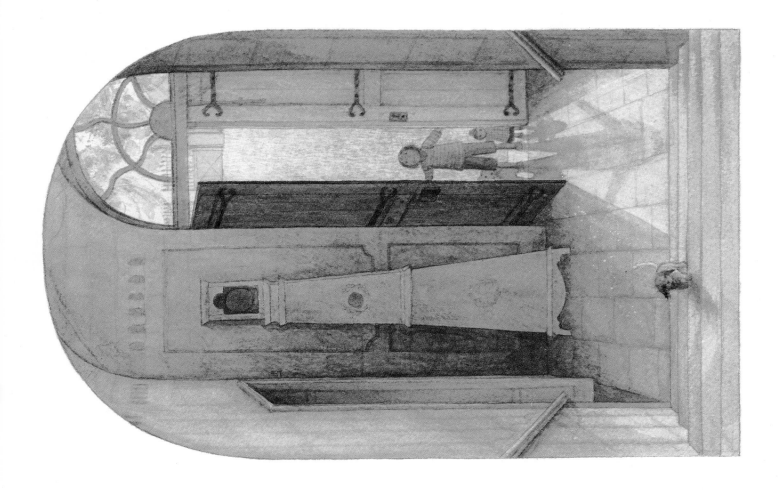

When they got to the castle, Nora pushed with all her might to open the heavy iron gates.

Creak!

Then she opened the big front door of the house.

Cr-r-reak!

In the hall the air was cold and damp.

"Hello!" she called out. "Is anyone at home?" But there was no reply. Brave Kiki trotted in and began to climb the stairs, and the others followed.

They came to a huge room. It was nearly empty, but on one wall was a painting of a man in armor. Was he a king? He looked so real that Nora instinctively bowed to him and said, "Excuse me, Your Highness, I hope we are not disturbing you."

The next room must have been the music room, for in it they found an old piano. It had lost some keys, and termites had eaten part of one of its legs, but it could still make music. Nora played a tune, and Maggie, Teddy and Kiki sang.

In a blue bedroom, they found a princess. "Princess, come and play with us," invited Nora, and Kiki wagged his tail as he looked at the lovely lady in the painting.

But the princess must have been shy, for she didn't reply, so the explorers left her there and started to climb up the inside of the tower. "What's up these stairs? Is anyone here?" asked Nora.

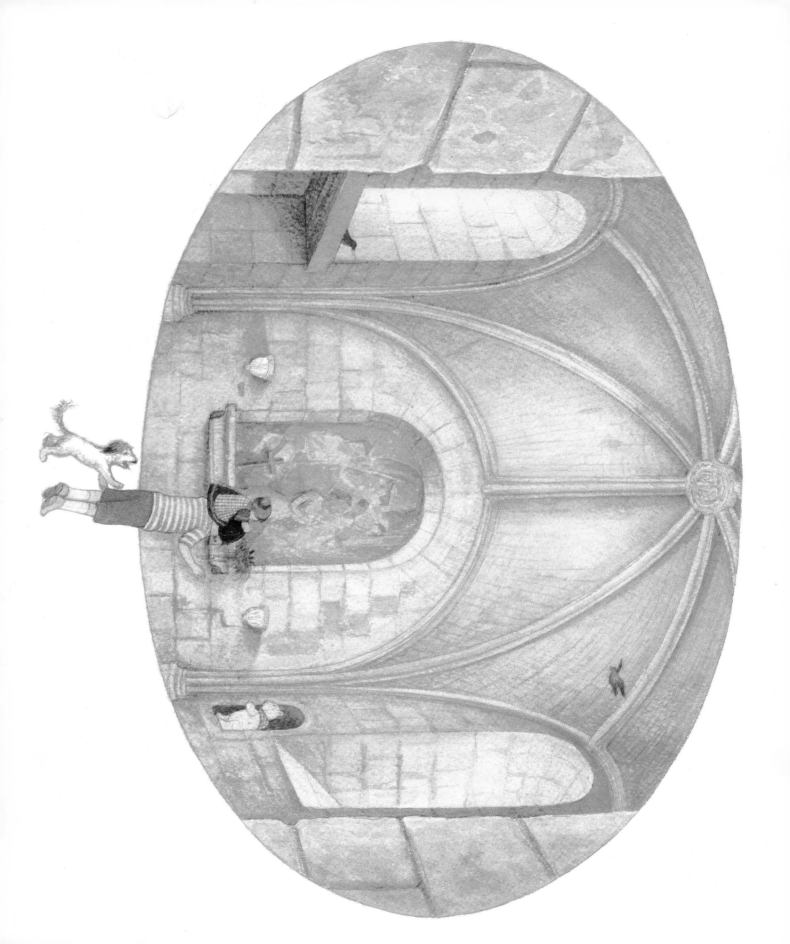

"Oh, look! There are some bluebirds. And some baby birds in a nest! They must be living here," she called to the others.

But Kiki was already on his way up some more stairs.

"Come on," said Nora to Maggie. "Let's see if there's anyone else up higher."

In the attic at the top of the stairs they found many trunks filled with old clothes, just right for dressing up in. Nora was trying on a pretty gown when—"Hello!" squeaked someone. It was a bat, hanging from a rafter. "Oh, you startled me," said Nora. "I guess you live in the castle, too. That gives me an idea . . ."

"Let's have a party in the castle tonight, and invite everyone who lives here!" she said. "Look, there's a lantern, and there are some musical instruments. *Tarantara!* Let's have some music while we look for some more guests."

"Look out the window!" said Nora. "There's a tower out there across the lawn. Maybe someone lives there."

Someone did. It was White Owl.

"Tarantara! Tra-la-la!"

"Who-o-o's that?"

White Owl liked to sleep in the daytime. Now she sounded quite angry.

"Oh, excuse us for waking you, White Owl. We just want to invite you to a party tonight. Will you come?"

"Thank you. As long as it's at night, I'd love to come. It's been a long time since there was a party here."

Now it was time to prepare for the party. From the tree outside the kitchen window they picked cherries until their basket overflowed.

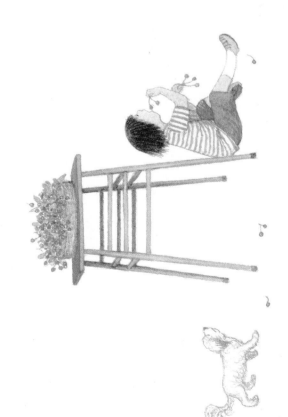

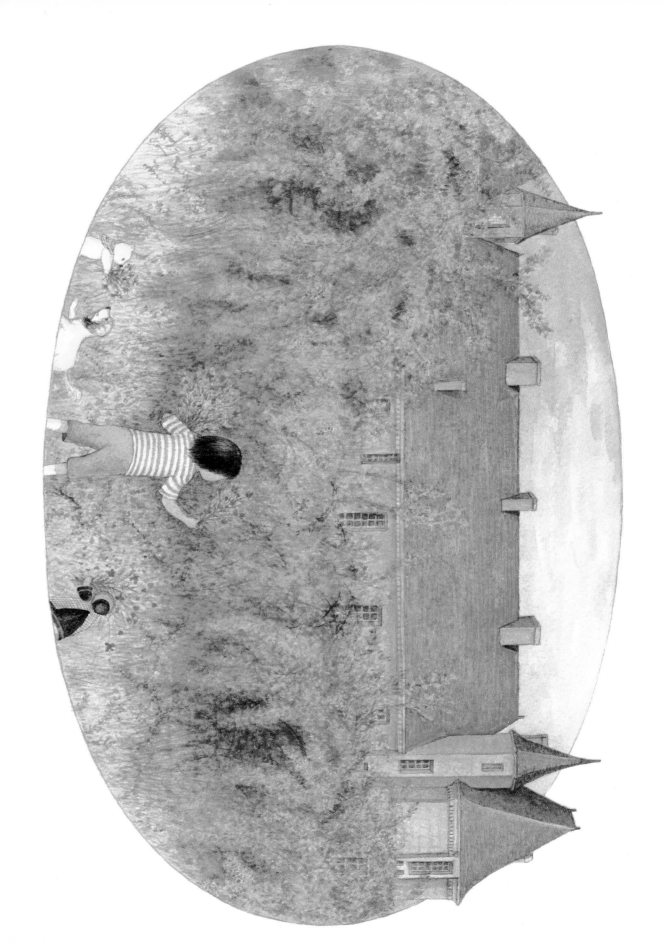

And in the field behind the castle they found hundreds of wildflowers.

"Oh, how beautiful!" said Nora. "Let's pick some for the party. All these colors will make the room look brighter."

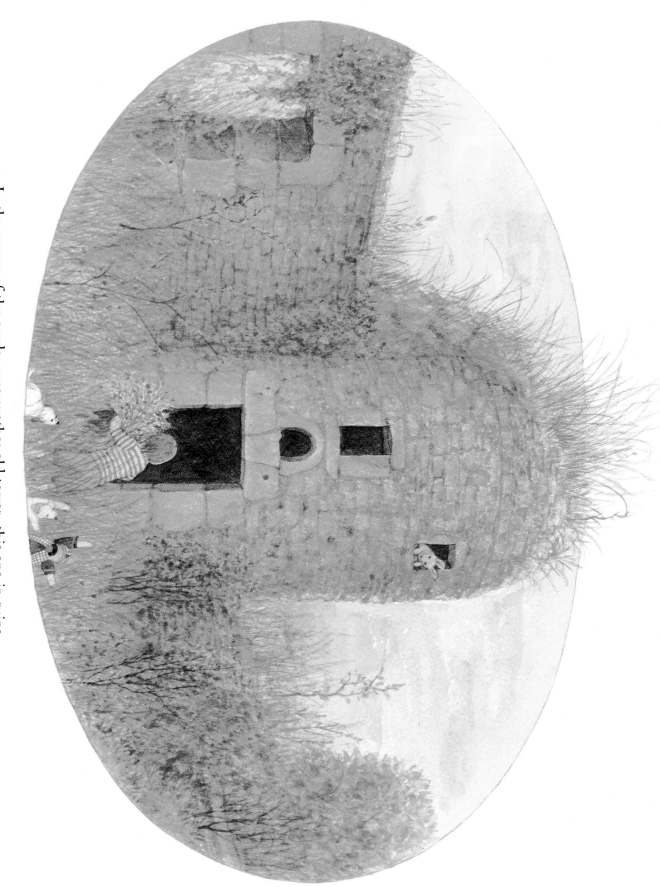

In the corner of the garden was another old tower, this one in ruins. "There must be someone here too," said Nora, running to the door. "Oh, look, there he is, up there. Mister Rabbit, will you come to our party tonight?"

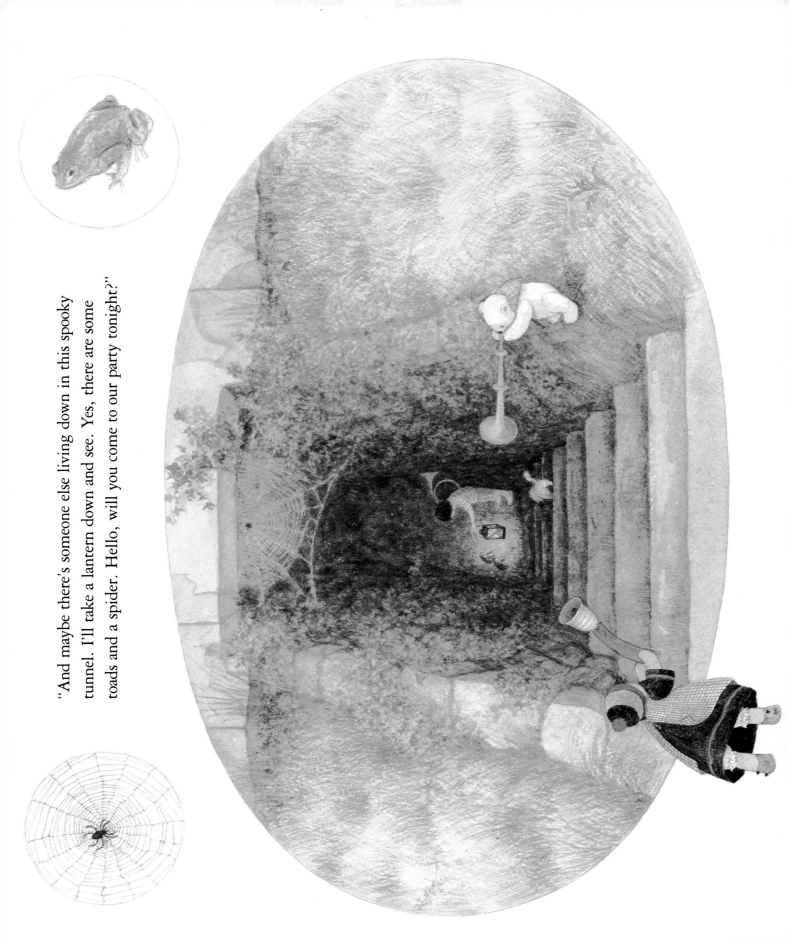

"And maybe there's someone else living down in this spooky tunnel. I'll take a lantern down and see. Yes, there are some toads and a spider. Hello, will you come to our party tonight?"

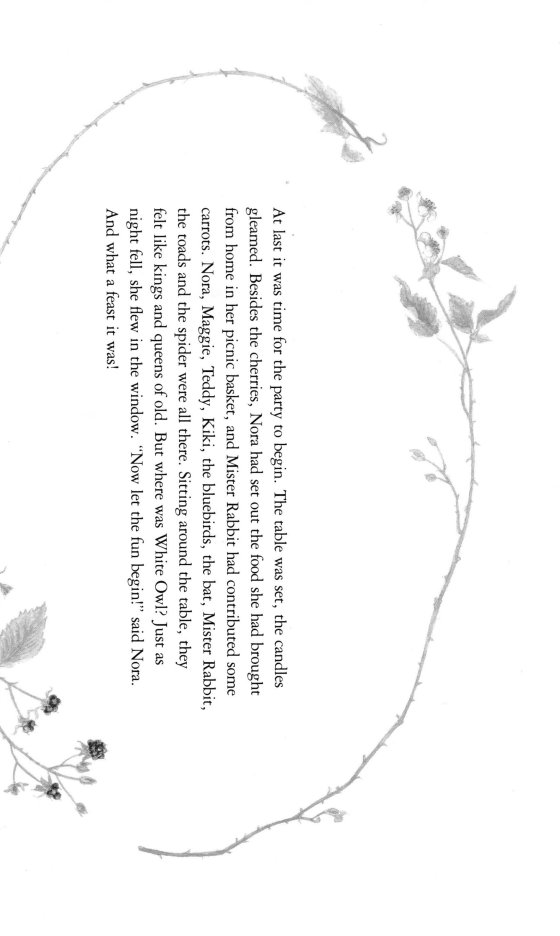

At last it was time for the party to begin. The table was set, the candles gleamed. Besides the cherries, Nora had set out the food she had brought from home in her picnic basket, and Mister Rabbit had contributed some carrots. Nora, Maggie, Teddy, Kiki, the bluebirds, the bat, Mister Rabbit, the toads and the spider were all there. Sitting around the table, they felt like kings and queens of old. But where was White Owl? Just as night fell, she flew in the window. "Now let the fun begin!" said Nora. And what a feast it was!

After eating their fill, they sang and danced in the moonlit garden. Towering against the night sky, the castle seemed to be smiling. Perhaps it was thinking back to the wonderful parties of centuries ago.

When the party was over, Nora and Maggie and Teddy and Kiki were too tired to think of going home. "You can sleep in my tower," said White Owl, who was still rather ashamed of having been so angry. So they snuggled together in the soft hay and soon fell fast asleep.

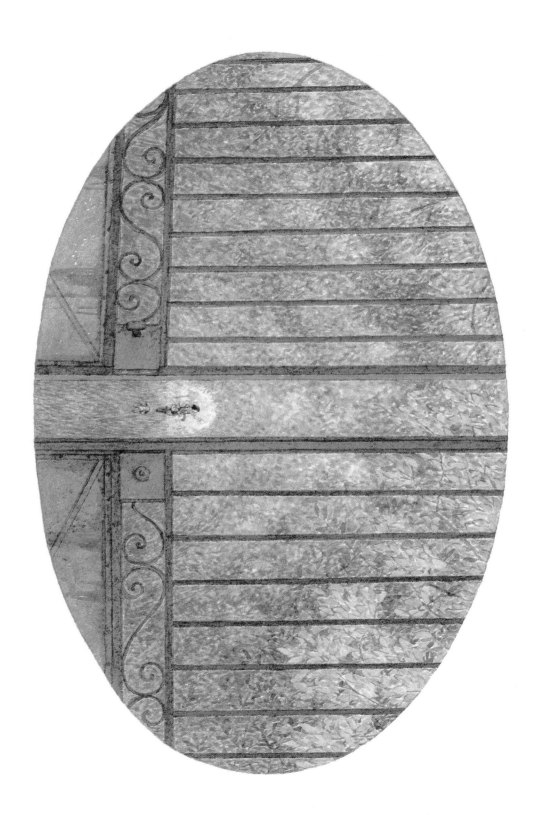

Early the next morning, Nora and the other brave explorers said goodbye to their new friends and set out for home. "We'll come back soon," she promised.

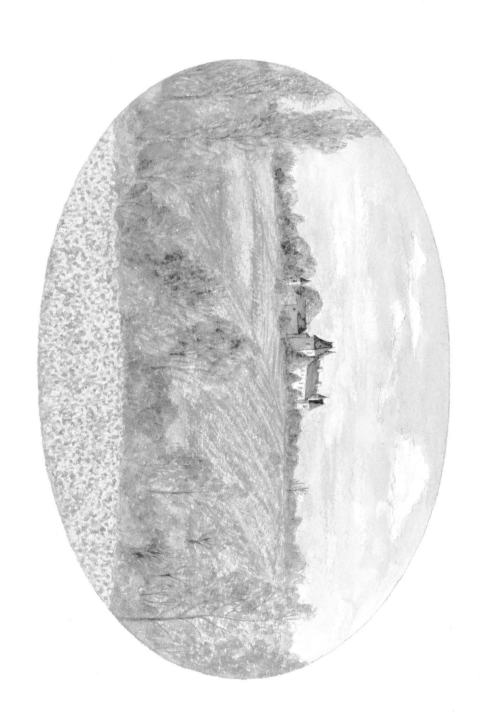

These days, when Nora looks out her window, she still sees the castle—
her castle. In the beautiful countryside, it looks as it always did, silent
and mysterious. But now, when the people of the village tell her that the
castle is deserted, Nora smiles and thinks fondly of all her friends who
live there. But she never tells anyone what she knows about the castle.
It is her secret.

These little mice missed the party! They didn't know about it until too late, because they were living in their summer homes, outside in the field. They only live in the castle in the wintertime. What a pity!

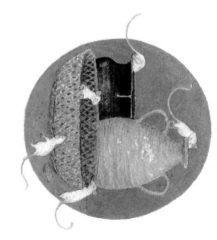

The publishers wish to thank Mr. Simon Piggott
for his valuable assistance in translating this story from the Japanese.

Copyright © 1984 by Satomi Ichikawa. Text translation copyright © 1986 by Philomel Books. First United States edition 1986, published by Philomel Books, a division of The Putnam Publishing Group, 51 Madison Avenue, New York, N.Y. 10010. All rights reserved. Except for use in a review, the reproduction or utilization of this work in any form or by any means is forbidden without the written permission of the publisher. Published simultaneously in Canada by General Publishing Company, Limited, Toronto. First published in Japan by Kaisei-sha, Ichigaya Tokyo. Translation rights were arranged with Kaisei-sha by the Japan Foreign Rights Centre. Printed in Hong Kong by South China Printing Co.

Library of Congress Cataloging in Publication Data: Ichikawa, Satomi. Nora's castle. Summary: Accompanied by her doll, Maggie, Teddy the stuffed bear, and Kiki the dog, a little girl sets out to explore the mysterious castle on the hill. [1. Castles—Fiction] I. Title. PZ7.I16No 1986 [E] 85-17293 ISBN 0-399-21302-3

First impression